Pooky Ate My Sneakers And Stole My Jeans

Pooky Ate My Sneakers
And Stole My Jeans

Written by

MARIA PSANIS

Illustrated by

DEMETRA BAKOGIORGAS

authorHOUSE®

AuthorHouse™ LLC
1663 Liberty Drive
Bloomington, IN 47403
www.authorhouse.com
Phone: 1-800-839-8640

Published by AuthorHouse   04/22/2014

ISBN: 978-1-4969-0632-8 (sc)
ISBN: 978-1-4969-0633-5 (e)

Library of Congress Control Number: 2014907526

DEDICATED TO...

Clara Canfield who is in heaven and to Bryanna, Hanna, Becky, and ella

and

To all our Sisters Living in Sisterhood

1

Pooky Ate My Sneakers
And Stole My Jeans

I ran inside the house. I was thirsty.
The soccer game was over. We had won.
I don't know why, but I'm not excited.
I'm exhausted!

Last night I stayed up doing homework
and reading books.
I think I like books.
At times books make me laugh
and other times books make me sad.
It depends on the story.
I have discovered the magic in books.
Yet I love soccer more.

I finally understand why my sister, Bella
loves books.
I'm not allowed to talk to her
when she's reading.
Now I understand why she doesn't
want to be interrupted.
She loses her concentration and
the continuation of the story.
I get it!

I grabbed a bottle of water from the refrigerator
and ran to my room.
I took off my sneakers and my jeans.
I sat on my bed.
It was hot!

This morning I had left my book
on top of my pillow.
When I reached out I realized
that there was something wrong.
Very wrong!
The book wasn't there.
I looked around. I frowned.
I stood up.

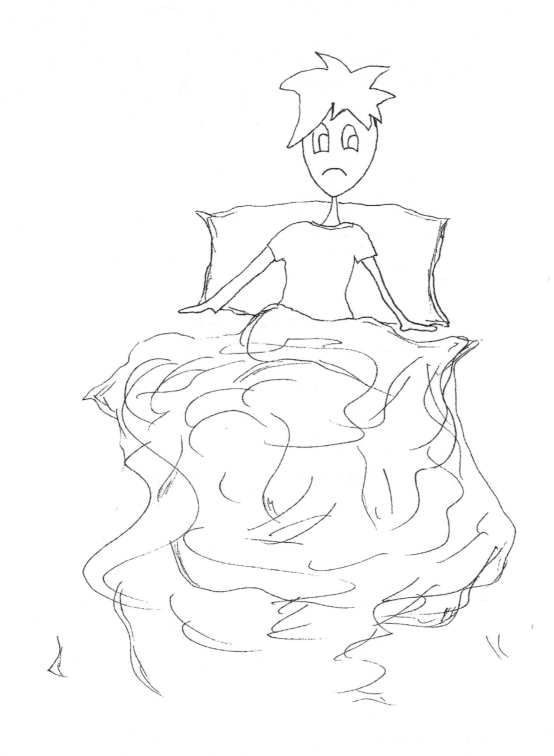

The book was nowhere to be seen.
I even looked in my closet.
I walked to the window. I looked around.
Not far from the door I saw pieces of papers.
I scratched my head.
No, no, no, something was wrong . . .

I found the book under my bed.
One corner was missing. It was chewed.
I opened the book. More pages were chewed.
I looked again around my room.
I jumped on the bed.
No, I wasn't scared. I was perplexed.
I grabbed the bottle of water
and ran downstairs.

"Mom"! I screamed.
"Mom where are you"?
She wasn't in the kitchen.
She wasn't in the family room.
I yelled for Bella.

Noah ran and jumped on me.

Noah is my little brother. He's six years old.

He told me that Bella was outside.

He told me that mom was working in her flower garden.

He asked me why I wasn't wearing my jeans.

I told him that it was hot.

My t-shirt covered my underwear.

He giggled.

I told Noah that there was something
or someone in our house
who liked to eat books.
His eyes almost popped out of his head.

He started laughing.
I told him that it wasn't funny.
I showed him the book.
He stopped laughing.
"I didn't do that"! He screamed and hugged me.
I told him to chill.
He asked me if we have monsters or ghosts
in our house.
I didn't have the answer.
He told me he was scared.

I asked him if he wanted to look around
the house with me to find
the monsters or the ghosts.
He told me no.
He was afraid.
I didn't make fun of him.
I told him not to worry,
I wasn't afraid.
I would protect him.

I was a little afraid too,
but I didn't tell Noah.
My dad has told me that it's
normal to have fear, but we
shouldn't allow ourselves
to be stuck in fear.
Do monsters exist?
How about ghosts?
Do I need to
look under every bed?

Noah wouldn't let go of me.
He was whispering in my ear.
He told me that he
didn't want the monsters and the
ghosts to hear him.
He wanted dad.
I told him that dad was at work.
He told me we can use his baseball bat to
chase the monsters away.
I agreed.

He jumped and ran to his room.
When he came back he was
holding his baseball bat.
"Here, you take it", he said handing it to me.
"I'll just stand behind you", he continued.
I smiled as I took the bat from him.

Noah and I tip-toed around the house.

Bella's voice startled us.
"Noah, mom wants you"! She screamed.
Noah ran outside.
I was holding the baseball bat.

Bella looked at me and made a funny face.
"What"? I said.
"Why aren't you wearing your jeans? And
where are your sneakers"? she asked,
shaking her head and rolling her eyes.
"You better not go outside like that
and embarrass me, and go
wear socks", she exclaimed.

Here we go again . . .
Bella never stops
telling me what to do and
how to do it.
She's all about image.

"Why are you holding Noah's baseball bat"? She asked.

I showed the book to her.

Bella accused me of being careless.

I told her that I don't chew books.

She took the book and was examining it.

"Do you think there's a creature

living in our house"? I asked her.

"This is very weird", she stated. "I need

to go and get mom. You didn't do this, right Sasha"?

She ran outside.

She looked scared.

Why wouldn't my sister believe me?
I think she's afraid just like Noah.
Am I the only brave one in this family?

Mom, Bella, and Noah marched inside.
Mom told me to put the baseball bat down.
She also told me to go and put on my jeans.
She looked at the book, than looked around.
I asked her if she was scared.
She said no.
"It could be a field mouse", she explained.

I ran to my room.
I closed the door behind me.
My jeans weren't on my bed.
One of my sneakers was missing.
I really don't like this, I thought.
I tip-toed in silence.
A mouse . . .
Can we have a mouse in our house?
I thought . . . .

My jeans suddenly appeared.
They were moving on the floor.
I looked at my legs than at my jeans.
I walked closer.
My jeans moved away from me.
I sat on the floor.
I tried not to make any noise.

My jeans rolled, skipped, danced,
pranced, glided.
I couldn't believe what I was seeing.
I scooted across the floor
not taking my eyes away from my jeans.
Can a mouse be under my jeans?
I didn't think so!
No way does a mouse have the ability
to take my jeans for a walk!
No way!

I hopped on my chair
and grabbed my socks.
My socks didn't match.
My jeans were sliding on the floor.
Do I dare to step on my jeans?

Abruptly I pounced on my jeans.
My jeans started to attack me.
I was thrown to the floor.
I looked around.
One of my sneakers was chewed.
I got mad.
No one eats my sneakers!
No one steals my jeans!
Is this some kind of a trick? I thought.

Amazing, my jeans were coming
closer to me.
Yikes!
Should I be scared?
Scared of my jeans?
I'm not scared of a mouse!
I called for my mom.
My jeans moved again, touching my feet.
I didn't move.
I didn't speak.

My eyes moved up and down, left and right.
My body was still.
My jeans moved up on my leg.
I held my breath.
My eyes got bigger.
I suddenly sneezed and out of my jeans
popped this long silver-gray snake.
It was big!
It was bigger than me.
I moved backwards.
He or she moved with me.
I think it's a male snake.

He got in my face.
My eyes didn't move.
I heard my heart beating loud.
Would he eat me? I thought.
Before I knew it he was hanging from
around my neck.
I think he's a friendly snake.
I tried to touch him but I was afraid
that he would bite me.

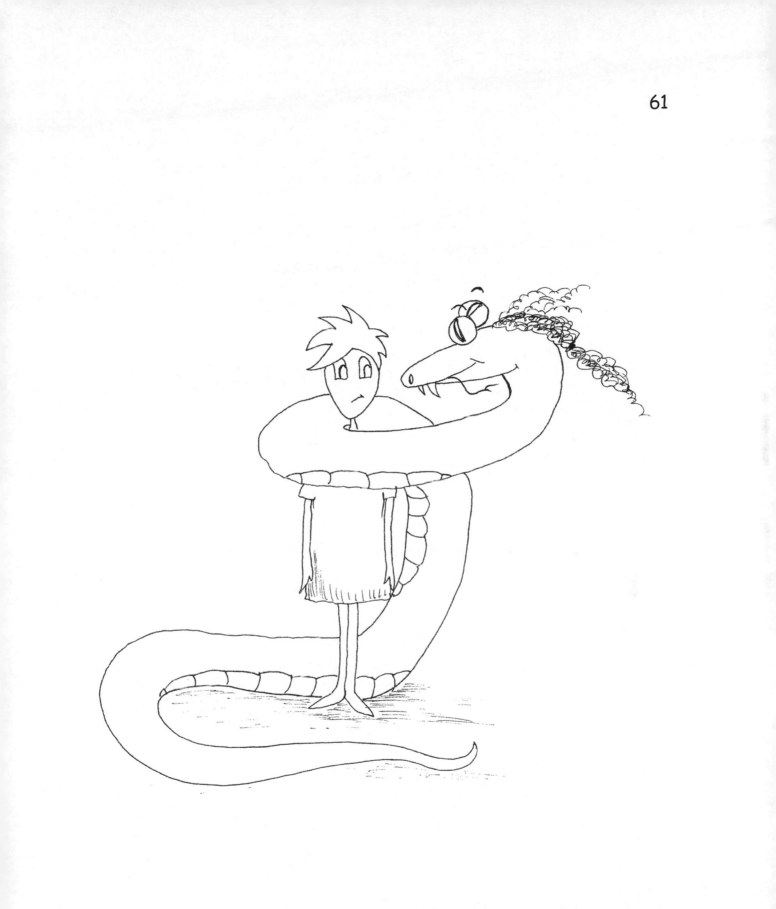

We stared in each other's eyes.

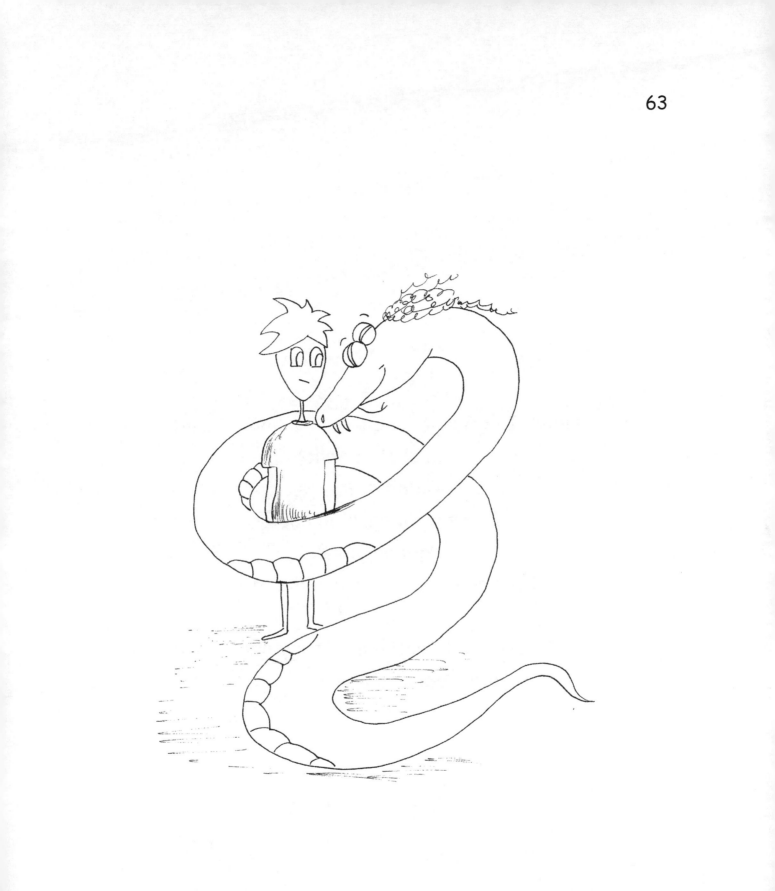

Hello, I'm Sasha, and who are you? I said.
Do snakes talk?
I didn't think so.
I think I'll call you Pooky.
Hello Pooky!
The snake was just looking at me.
I smiled.
Slowly I took him off my neck
and placed him on my bed.

"Pooky why did you eat my sneaker"? I said,
as I was putting my jeans on." Were
you trying to steal my jeans"?
He just looked at me puzzled.
I wondered if he understood what I was saying to him.
What was he thinking?

Just then the door opened.
Pooky glided on me and twisted
himself around my neck.
Bella freaked out.
She started screaming for mom.
She ran out of the room.
I just looked at Pooky and smiled.

Mom, Bella, and Noah appeared in my room.
Noah was holding the baseball bat.
Bella was hiding behind mom.
Mom was speechless.
"Wow, a snake, a big snake", Noah yelled.
"I like snakes"! He was excited.

"This is my family", I whispered to Pooky.
"Don't be afraid. We all love animals".
I didn't think my mom liked seeing Pooky on me,
or in our house.

"Sasha take him outside", mom demanded.
"But mom he's a friendly snake. His name is Pooky.
I named him.
Can we keep him?
Please . . . ."
I pleaded.

"Can I touch him"? Noah said, coming closer.
"I'm not touching him"! Bella vehemently voiced.
"Sasha you need to take Pooky outside", mom exclaimed.
"But mom . . ." I said.
"No buts, Sasha", she firmly stated. "Outside"!
She pointed to the door.

My mom made me take Pooky outside.
"He needs to be free". Mom told me.

Pooky slithered down from my body
and into the woods he went.
He looked back once, stretching his head up
he stuck his tongue out.
Was he making fun of me?
or was he saying goodbye?
I will never know.
Just then I heard my dog, Lady Love barking.

I'll need new sneakers, I thought.
Lady Love ran and jumped on me.
She licked my face.
"Come girl, let's go inside", I said.
"You'll never have the chance to be
friends with Pooky all because of mom,
but it's okay, Pooky is free", I said,
giving my dog a hug.